11/08

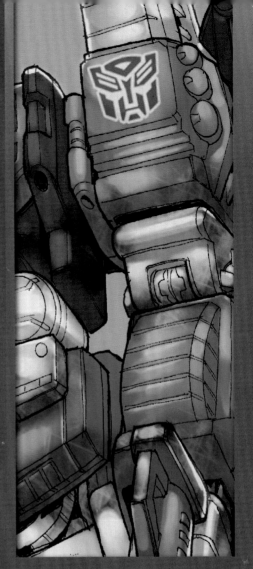

Even in war, there are codes of conduct that must be abided by and, when there are transgressions, enforced. In this respect, he is the law. Though an AUTOBOT by allegiance, he fulfils a largely autonomous role, investigating, assessing and— if necessary—punishing those who cross the line drawn in the sand. His name is…

… ULTRA MAGNUS.

THE TRANSFORMERS: SPOTLIGHT:
ULTRA MAGNUS

WRITTEN BY: SIMON FURMAN

ART BY: ROBBY MUSSO

COLORS BY: KIERAN OATS

COVER ART BY: KLAUS SCHERWINSKI
& ROBBY MUSSO

LETTERS BY: NEIL UYETAKE

EDITS BY: CHRIS RYALL & DAN TAYLOR

Licensed by:
Hasbro Properties Group

Special thanks to Hasbro's Aaron Archer, Elizabeth Griffin, Amié Lozanski, and Richard Zambarano for their invaluable assistance.

Spotlight

VISIT US AT
www.abdopublishing.com

Reinforced library bound edition published in 2008 by Spotlight, a division of the ABDO Publishing Group, 8000 West 78th Street, Edina, Minnesota 55439. Published by agreement with IDW Publishing. www.idwpublishing.com

Library of Congress Cataloging-in-Publication Data

Furman, Simon.
  Ultra Magnus / written by Simon Furman ; art by Robby Musso ; colors by Kieran Oats ; cover art by Klaus Scherwinski & Robby Musso ; letters by Neil Uyetake. -- Reinforced library bound ed.
      p. cm. -- (Transformers: Spotlight)
  ISBN 978-1-59961-479-3 (lib. bdg.)
  1. Graphic novels. I. Musso, Robby. II. Oats, Kieran. III. Title.

PN6727.F87U48 2008
741.5'973--dc22

                                                                2007033987

All Spotlight books have reinforced library bindings and are manufactured in the United States of America.

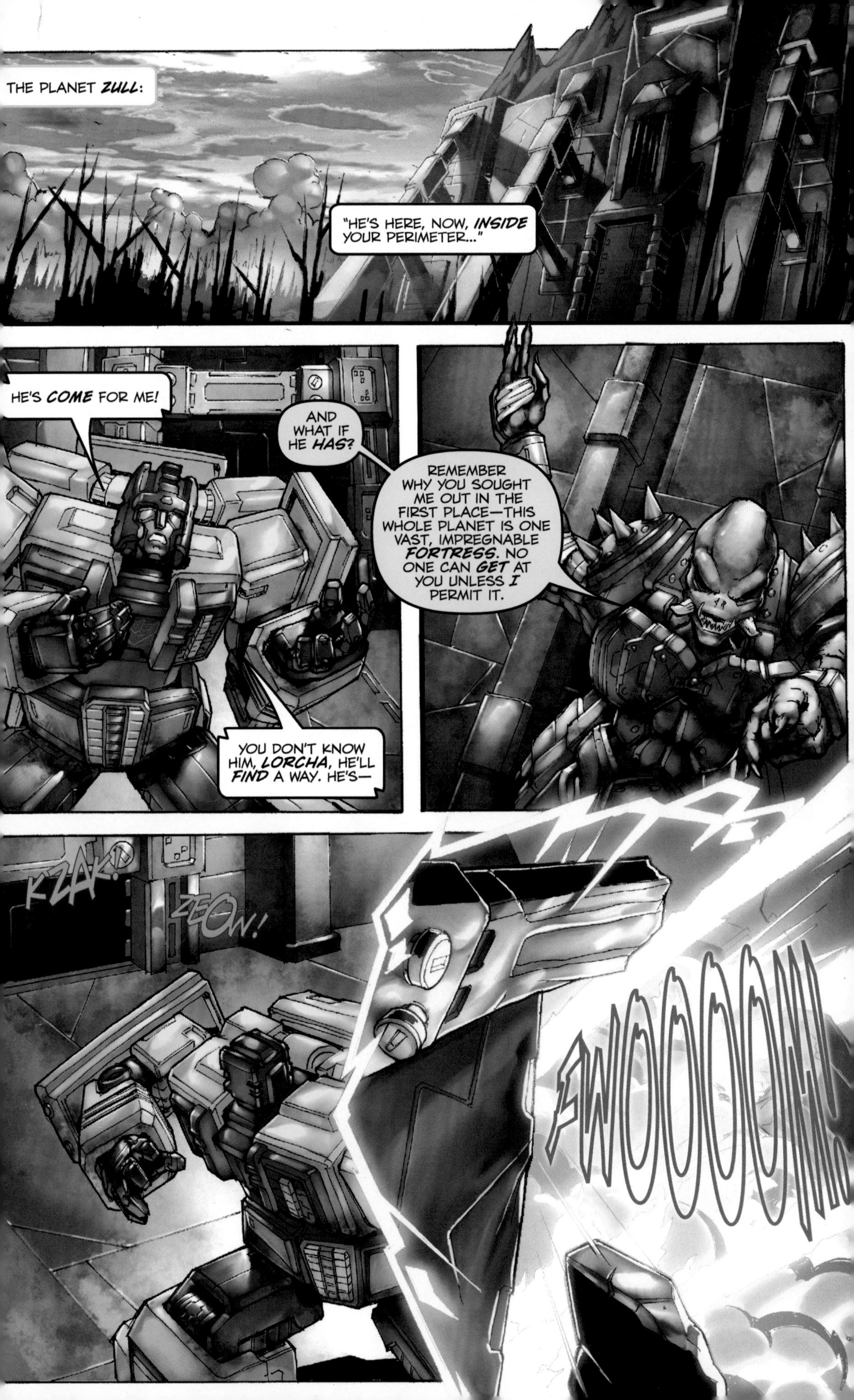
THE PLANET ZULL:
"HE'S HERE, NOW, INSIDE YOUR PERIMETER..."
HE'S COME FOR ME!
AND WHAT IF HE HAS?
REMEMBER WHY YOU SOUGHT ME OUT IN THE FIRST PLACE—THIS WHOLE PLANET IS ONE VAST, IMPREGNABLE FORTRESS. NO ONE CAN GET AT YOU UNLESS I PERMIT IT.
YOU DON'T KNOW HIM, LORCHA, HE'LL FIND A WAY. HE'S—
KZAK!
ZEOW!
FWOOOOM!

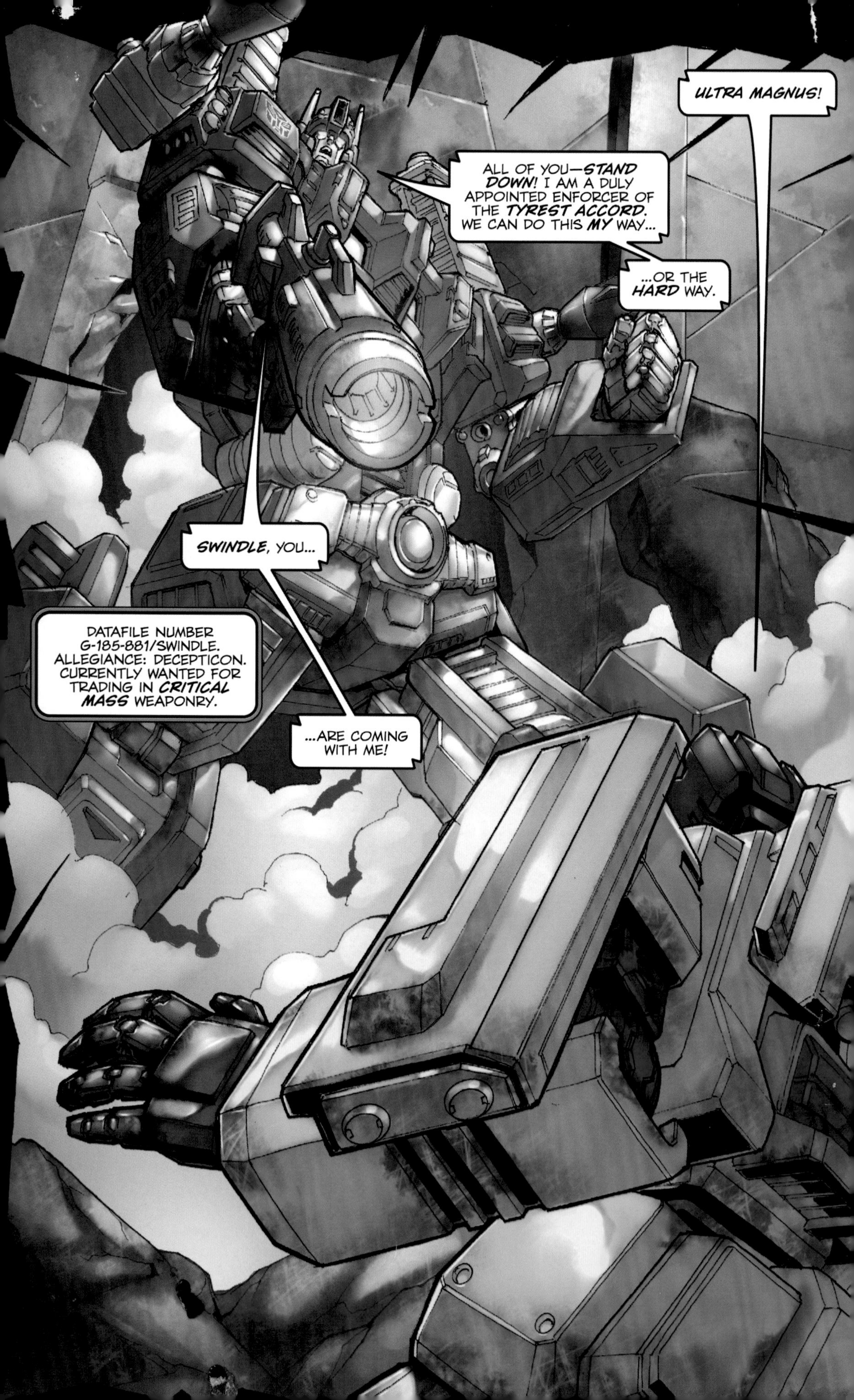
ULTRA MAGNUS!
ALL OF YOU—STAND DOWN! I AM A DULY APPOINTED ENFORCER OF THE TYREST ACCORD. WE CAN DO THIS MY WAY...
...OR THE HARD WAY.
SWINDLE, YOU...
DATAFILE NUMBER G-185-881/SWINDLE. ALLEGIANCE: DECEPTICON. CURRENTLY WANTED FOR TRADING IN CRITICAL MASS WEAPONRY.
...ARE COMING WITH ME!

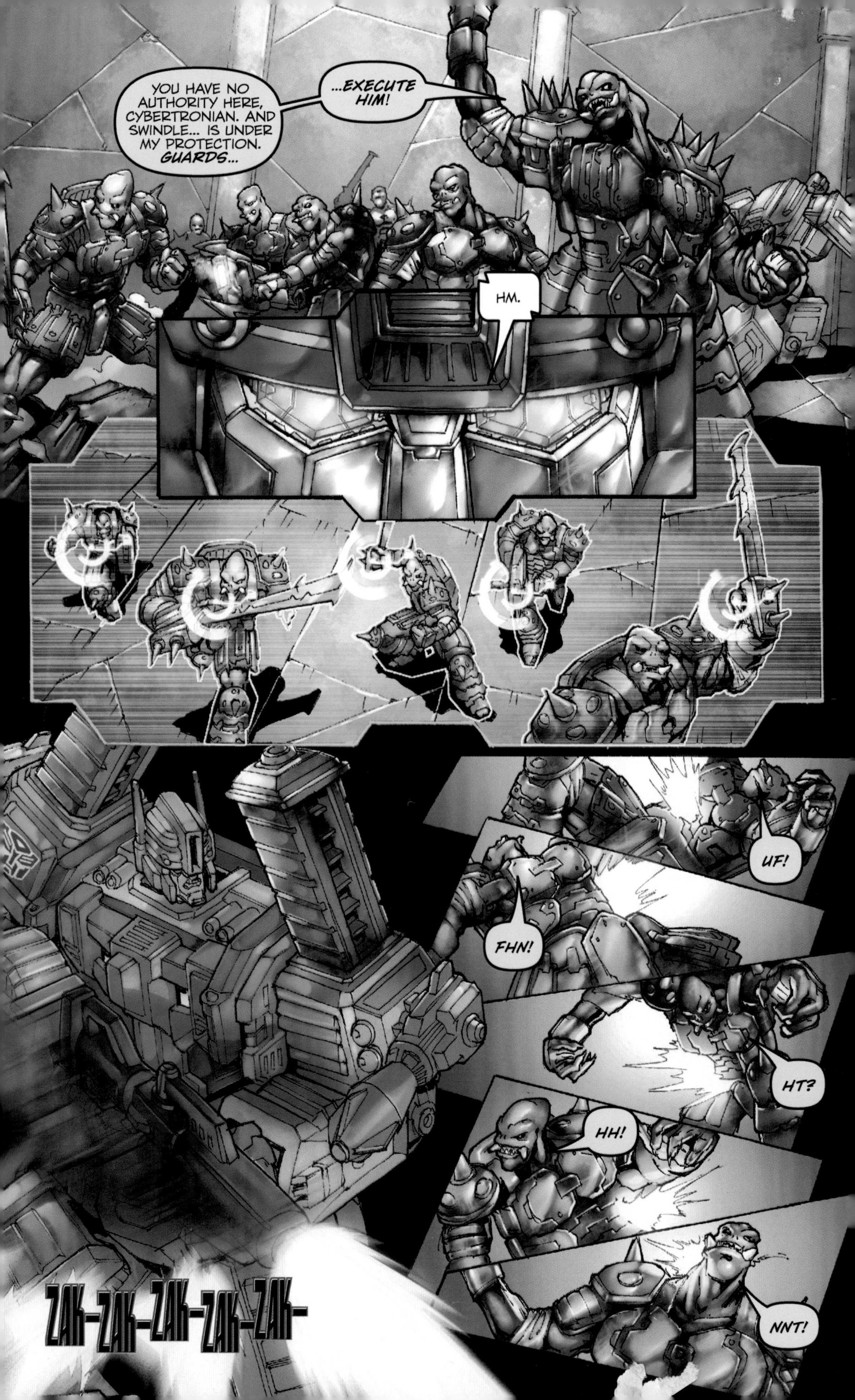
YOU HAVE NO AUTHORITY HERE, CYBERTRONIAN. AND SWINDLE... IS UNDER MY PROTECTION. GUARDS...
...EXECUTE HIM!
HM.
UF!
FHN!
HT?
HH!
ZAK-ZAK-ZAK-ZAK-ZAK-
NNT!

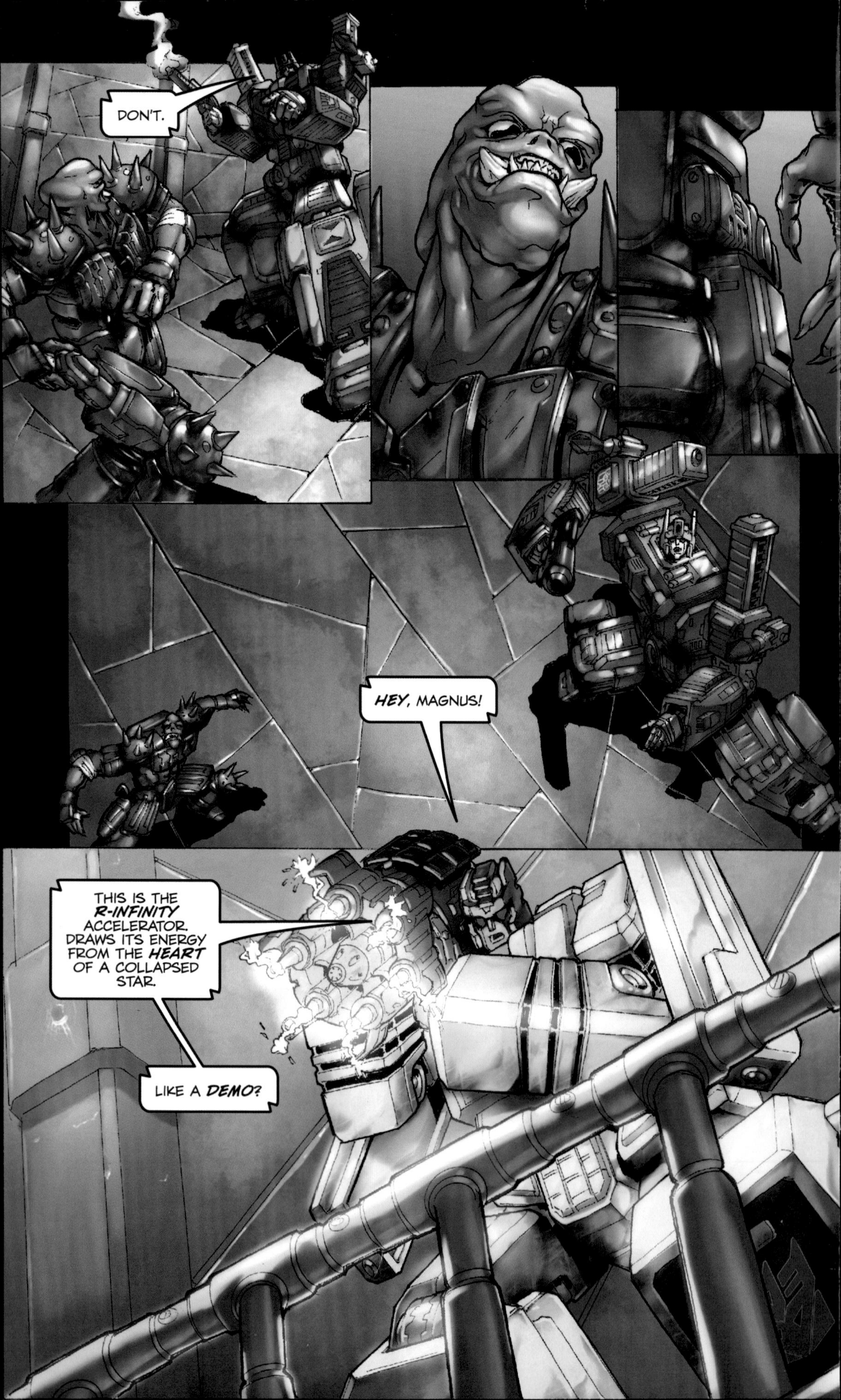
DON'T.
HEY, MAGNUS!
THIS IS THE R-INFINITY ACCELERATOR. DRAWS ITS ENERGY FROM THE HEART OF A COLLAPSED STAR.
LIKE A DEMO?

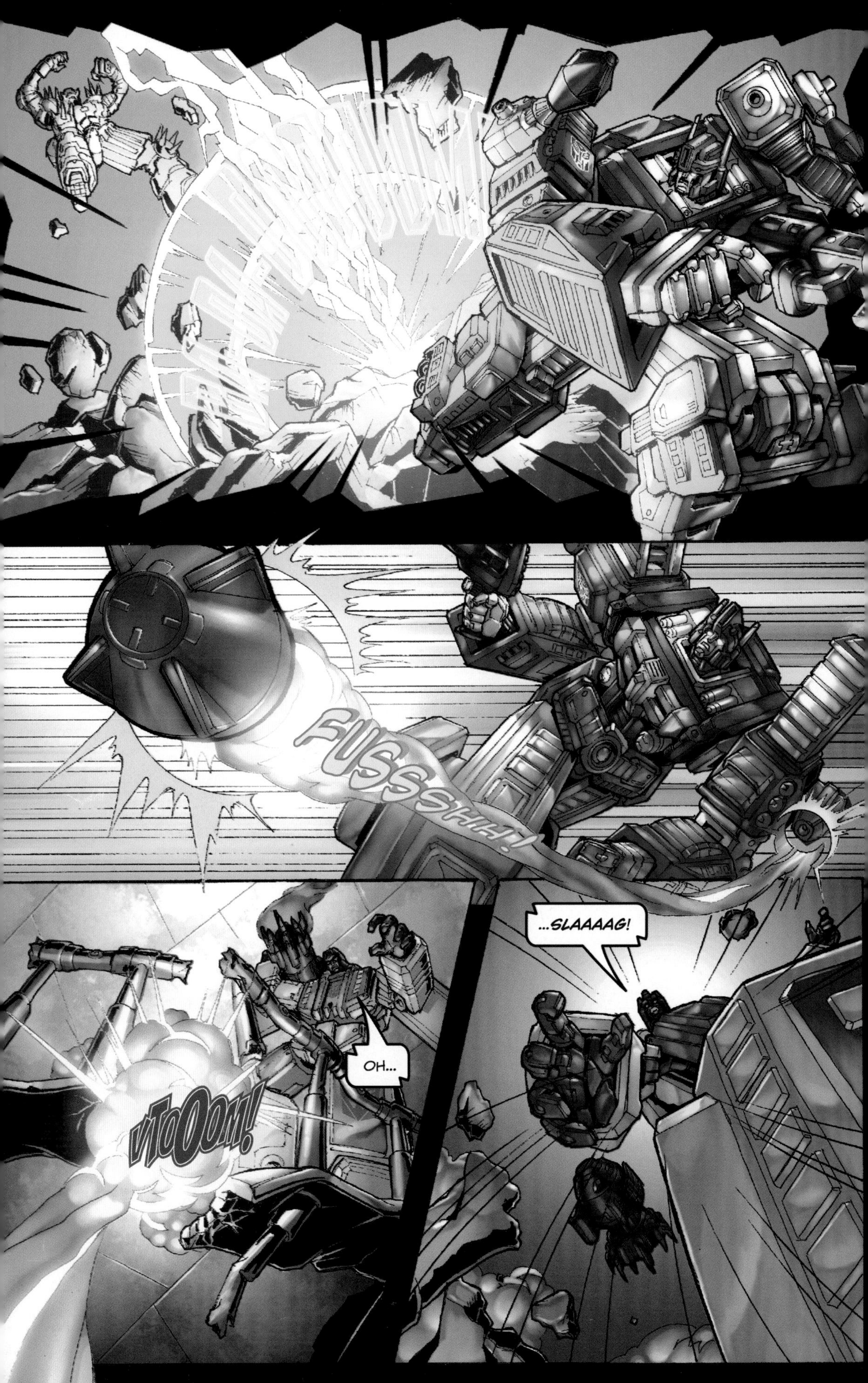
FUSSSHH!
VTOOOM!
OH...
...SLAAAAG!

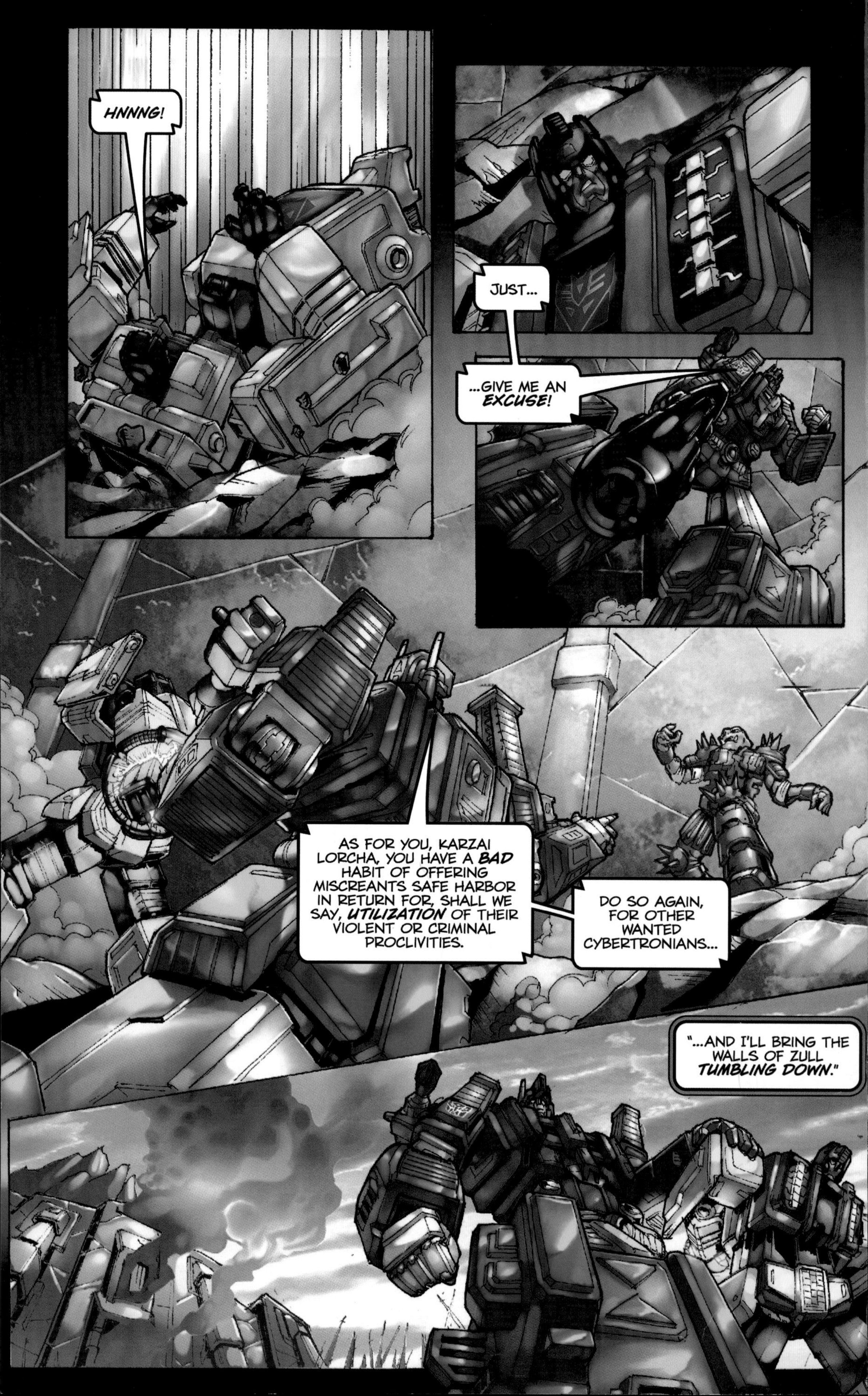
HNNNG!
JUST...
...GIVE ME AN EXCUSE!
AS FOR YOU, KARZAI LORCHA, YOU HAVE A BAD HABIT OF OFFERING MISCREANTS SAFE HARBOR IN RETURN FOR, SHALL WE SAY, UTILIZATION OF THEIR VIOLENT OR CRIMINAL PROCLIVITIES.
DO SO AGAIN, FOR OTHER WANTED CYBERTRONIANS...
"...AND I'LL BRING THE WALLS OF ZULL TUMBLING DOWN."

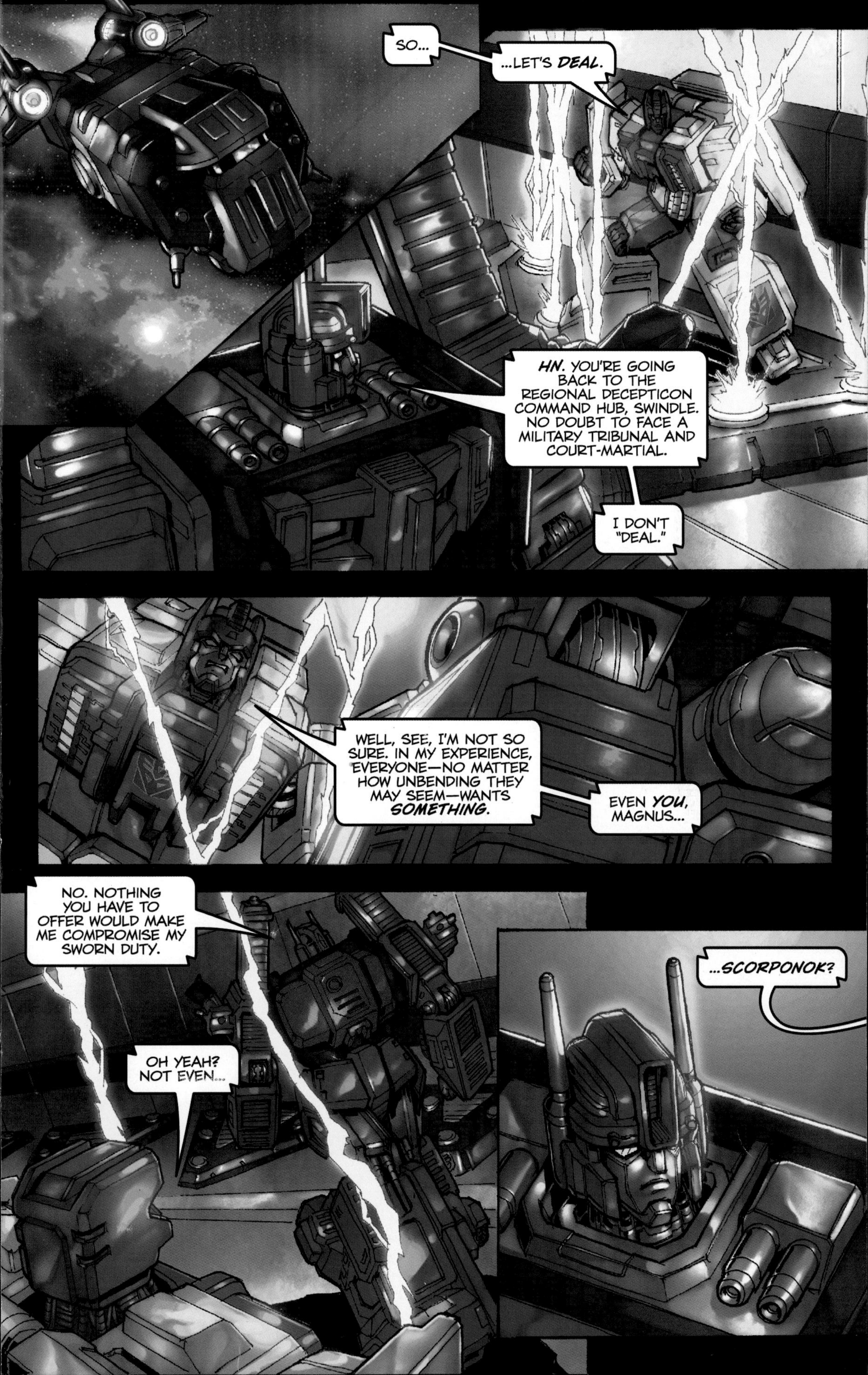
SO...
...LET'S DEAL.
HN. YOU'RE GOING BACK TO THE REGIONAL DECEPTICON COMMAND HUB, SWINDLE. NO DOUBT TO FACE A MILITARY TRIBUNAL AND COURT-MARTIAL.
I DON'T "DEAL."
WELL, SEE, I'M NOT SO SURE. IN MY EXPERIENCE, EVERYONE—NO MATTER HOW UNBENDING THEY MAY SEEM—WANTS SOMETHING.
EVEN YOU, MAGNUS...
NO. NOTHING YOU HAVE TO OFFER WOULD MAKE ME COMPROMISE MY SWORN DUTY.
OH YEAH? NOT EVEN...
...SCORPONOK?

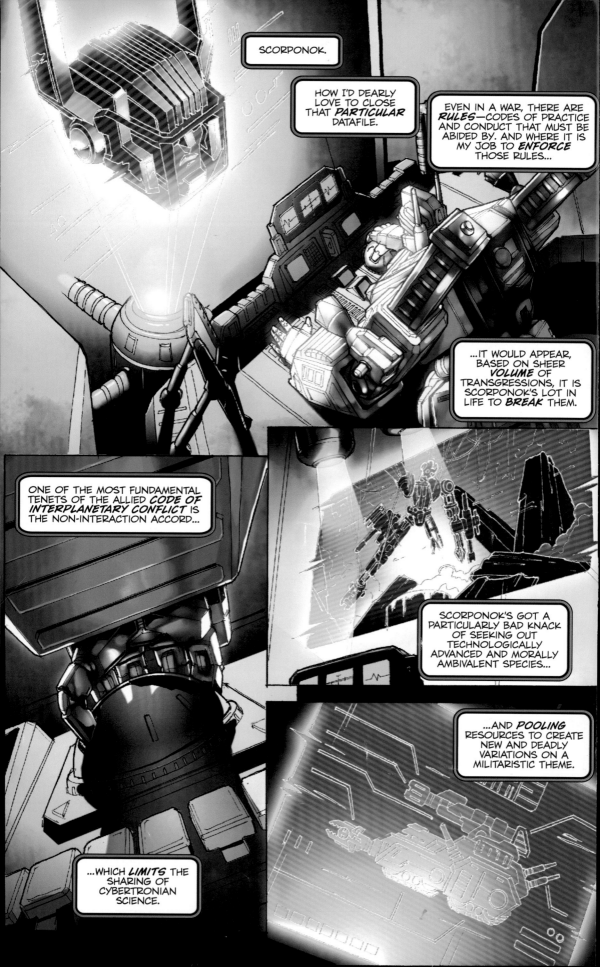

SCORPONOK.

HOW I'D DEARLY LOVE TO CLOSE THAT *PARTICULAR* DATAFILE.

EVEN IN A WAR, THERE ARE *RULES*—CODES OF PRACTICE AND CONDUCT THAT MUST BE ABIDED BY. AND WHERE IT IS MY JOB TO *ENFORCE* THOSE RULES...

...IT WOULD APPEAR, BASED ON SHEER *VOLUME* OF TRANSGRESSIONS, IT IS SCORPONOK'S LOT IN LIFE TO *BREAK* THEM.

ONE OF THE MOST FUNDAMENTAL TENETS OF THE ALLIED *CODE OF INTERPLANETARY CONFLICT* IS THE NON-INTERACTION ACCORD...

SCORPONOK'S GOT A PARTICULARLY BAD KNACK OF SEEKING OUT TECHNOLOGICALLY ADVANCED AND MORALLY AMBIVALENT SPECIES...

...AND *POOLING* RESOURCES TO CREATE NEW AND DEADLY VARIATIONS ON A MILITARISTIC THEME.

...WHICH *LIMITS* THE SHARING OF CYBERTRONIAN SCIENCE.

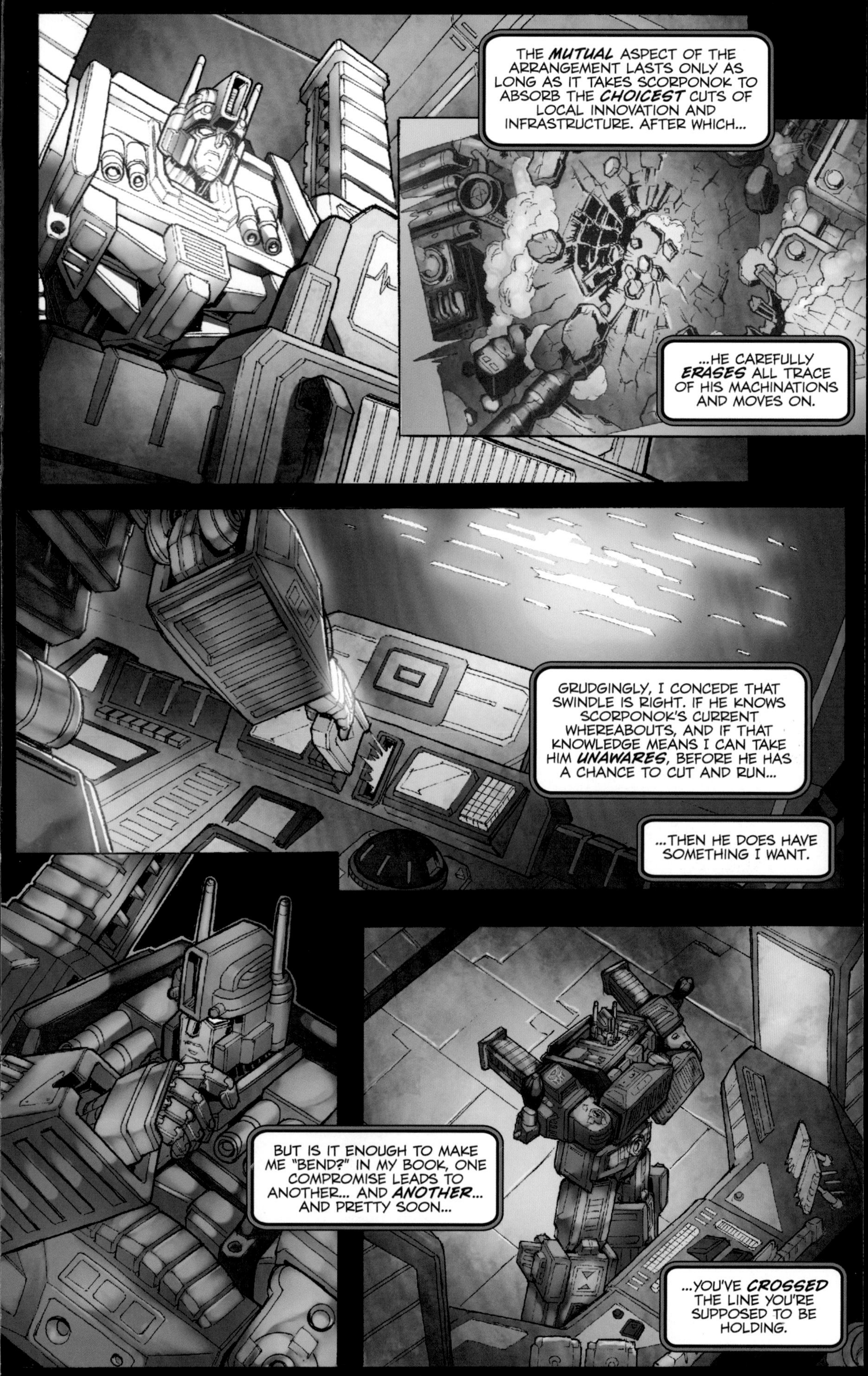
THE MUTUAL ASPECT OF THE ARRANGEMENT LASTS ONLY AS LONG AS IT TAKES SCORPONOK TO ABSORB THE CHOICEST CUTS OF LOCAL INNOVATION AND INFRASTRUCTURE. AFTER WHICH...
...HE CAREFULLY ERASES ALL TRACE OF HIS MACHINATIONS AND MOVES ON.
GRUDGINGLY, I CONCEDE THAT SWINDLE IS RIGHT. IF HE KNOWS SCORPONOK'S CURRENT WHEREABOUTS, AND IF THAT KNOWLEDGE MEANS I CAN TAKE HIM UNAWARES, BEFORE HE HAS A CHANCE TO CUT AND RUN...
...THEN HE DOES HAVE SOMETHING I WANT.
BUT IS IT ENOUGH TO MAKE ME "BEND?" IN MY BOOK, ONE COMPROMISE LEADS TO ANOTHER... AND ANOTHER... AND PRETTY SOON...
...YOU'VE CROSSED THE LINE YOU'RE SUPPOSED TO BE HOLDING.

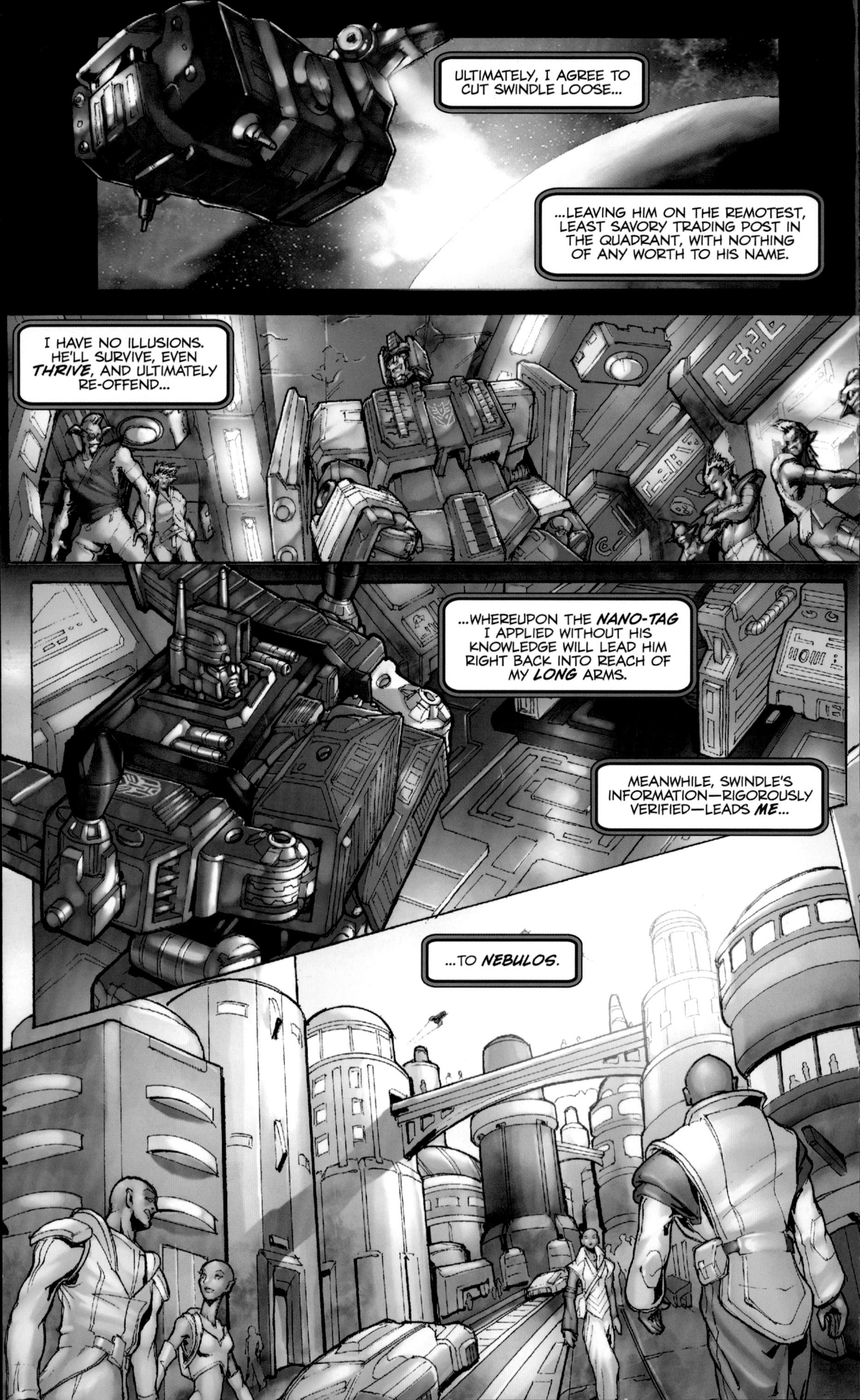
ULTIMATELY, I AGREE TO CUT SWINDLE LOOSE...
...LEAVING HIM ON THE REMOTEST, LEAST SAVORY TRADING POST IN THE QUADRANT, WITH NOTHING OF ANY WORTH TO HIS NAME.
I HAVE NO ILLUSIONS. HE'LL SURVIVE, EVEN *THRIVE*, AND ULTIMATELY RE-OFFEND...
...WHEREUPON THE *NANO-TAG* I APPLIED WITHOUT HIS KNOWLEDGE WILL LEAD HIM RIGHT BACK INTO REACH OF MY *LONG* ARMS.
MEANWHILE, SWINDLE'S INFORMATION—RIGOROUSLY VERIFIED—LEADS *ME*...
...TO *NEBULOS*.

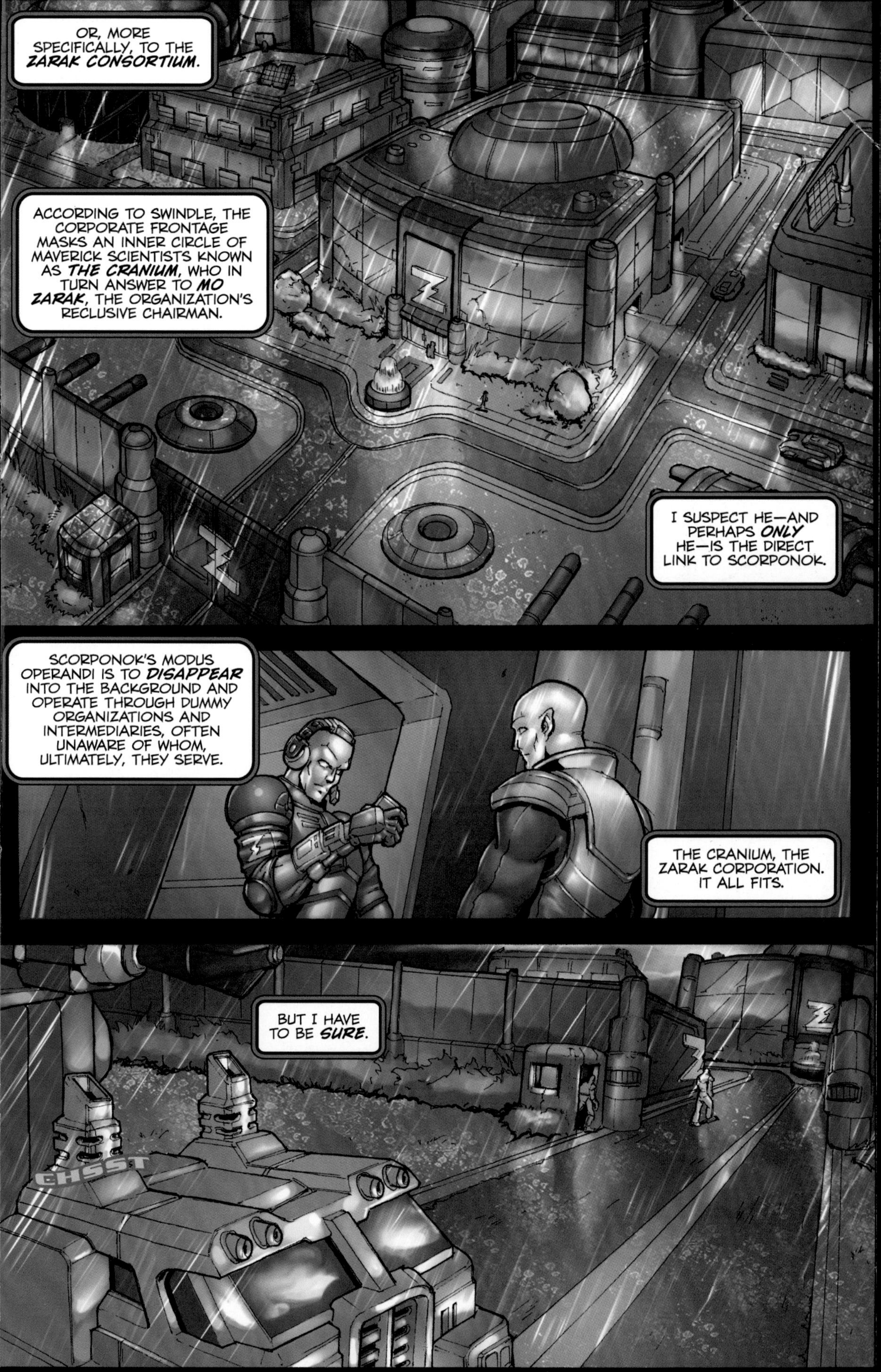
OR, MORE SPECIFICALLY, TO THE ZARAK CONSORTIUM.
ACCORDING TO SWINDLE, THE CORPORATE FRONTAGE MASKS AN INNER CIRCLE OF MAVERICK SCIENTISTS KNOWN AS THE CRANIUM, WHO IN TURN ANSWER TO MO ZARAK, THE ORGANIZATION'S RECLUSIVE CHAIRMAN.
I SUSPECT HE—AND PERHAPS ONLY HE—IS THE DIRECT LINK TO SCORPONOK.
SCORPONOK'S MODUS OPERANDI IS TO DISAPPEAR INTO THE BACKGROUND AND OPERATE THROUGH DUMMY ORGANIZATIONS AND INTERMEDIARIES, OFTEN UNAWARE OF WHOM, ULTIMATELY, THEY SERVE.
THE CRANIUM, THE ZARAK CORPORATION. IT ALL FITS.
BUT I HAVE TO BE SURE.

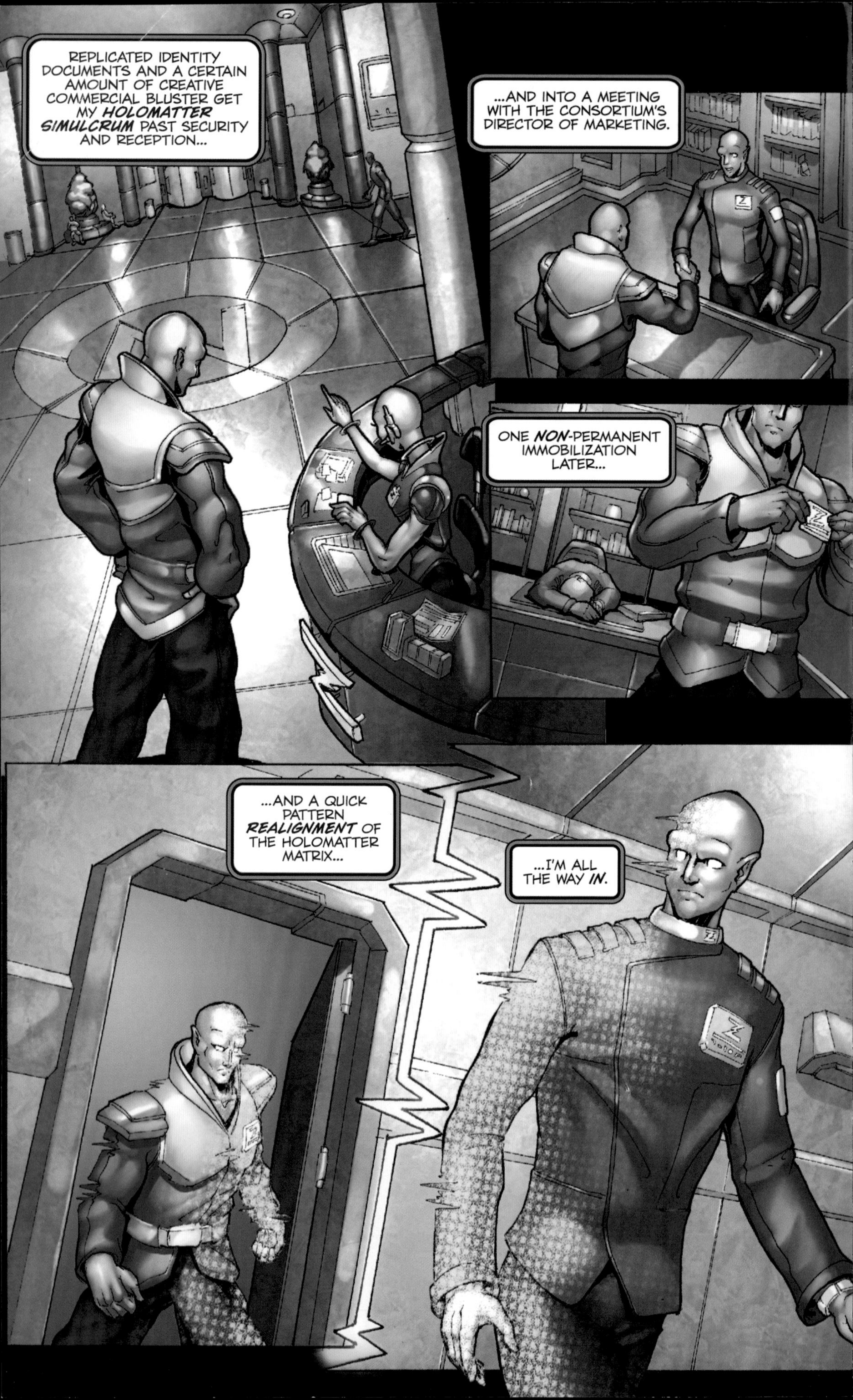
REPLICATED IDENTITY DOCUMENTS AND A CERTAIN AMOUNT OF CREATIVE COMMERCIAL BLUSTER GET MY HOLOMATTER SIMULCRUM PAST SECURITY AND RECEPTION...
...AND INTO A MEETING WITH THE CONSORTIUM'S DIRECTOR OF MARKETING.
ONE NON-PERMANENT IMMOBILIZATION LATER...
...AND A QUICK PATTERN REALIGNMENT OF THE HOLOMATTER MATRIX...
...I'M ALL THE WAY IN.

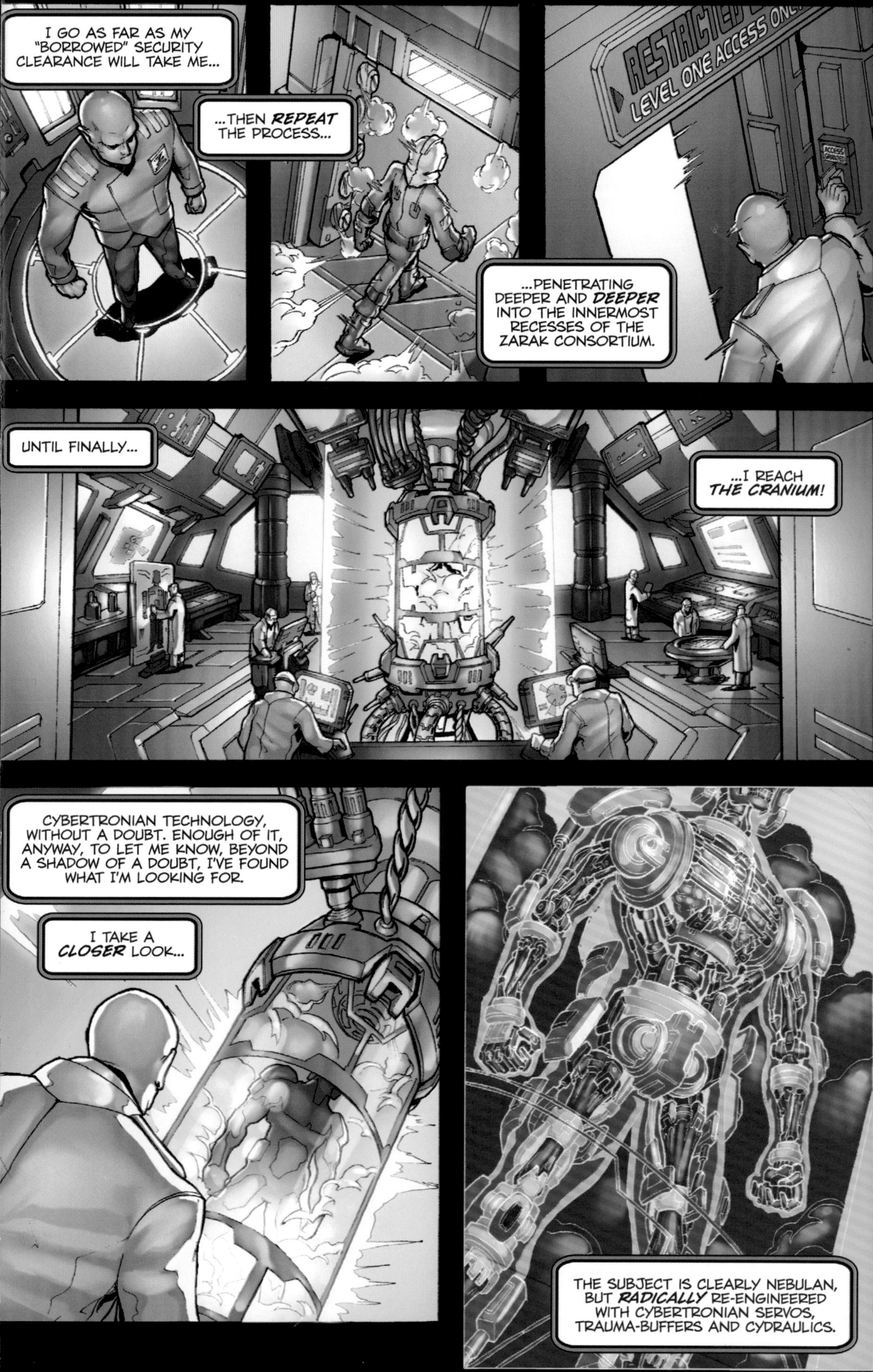
I GO AS FAR AS MY "BORROWED" SECURITY CLEARANCE WILL TAKE ME...
...THEN REPEAT THE PROCESS...
RESTRICTED
LEVEL ONE ACCESS
...PENETRATING DEEPER AND DEEPER INTO THE INNERMOST RECESSES OF THE ZARAK CONSORTIUM.
UNTIL FINALLY...
...I REACH THE CRANIUM!
CYBERTRONIAN TECHNOLOGY, WITHOUT A DOUBT. ENOUGH OF IT, ANYWAY, TO LET ME KNOW, BEYOND A SHADOW OF A DOUBT, I'VE FOUND WHAT I'M LOOKING FOR.
I TAKE A CLOSER LOOK...
THE SUBJECT IS CLEARLY NEBULAN, BUT RADICALLY RE-ENGINEERED WITH CYBERTRONIAN SERVOS, TRAUMA-BUFFERS AND CYDRAULICS.

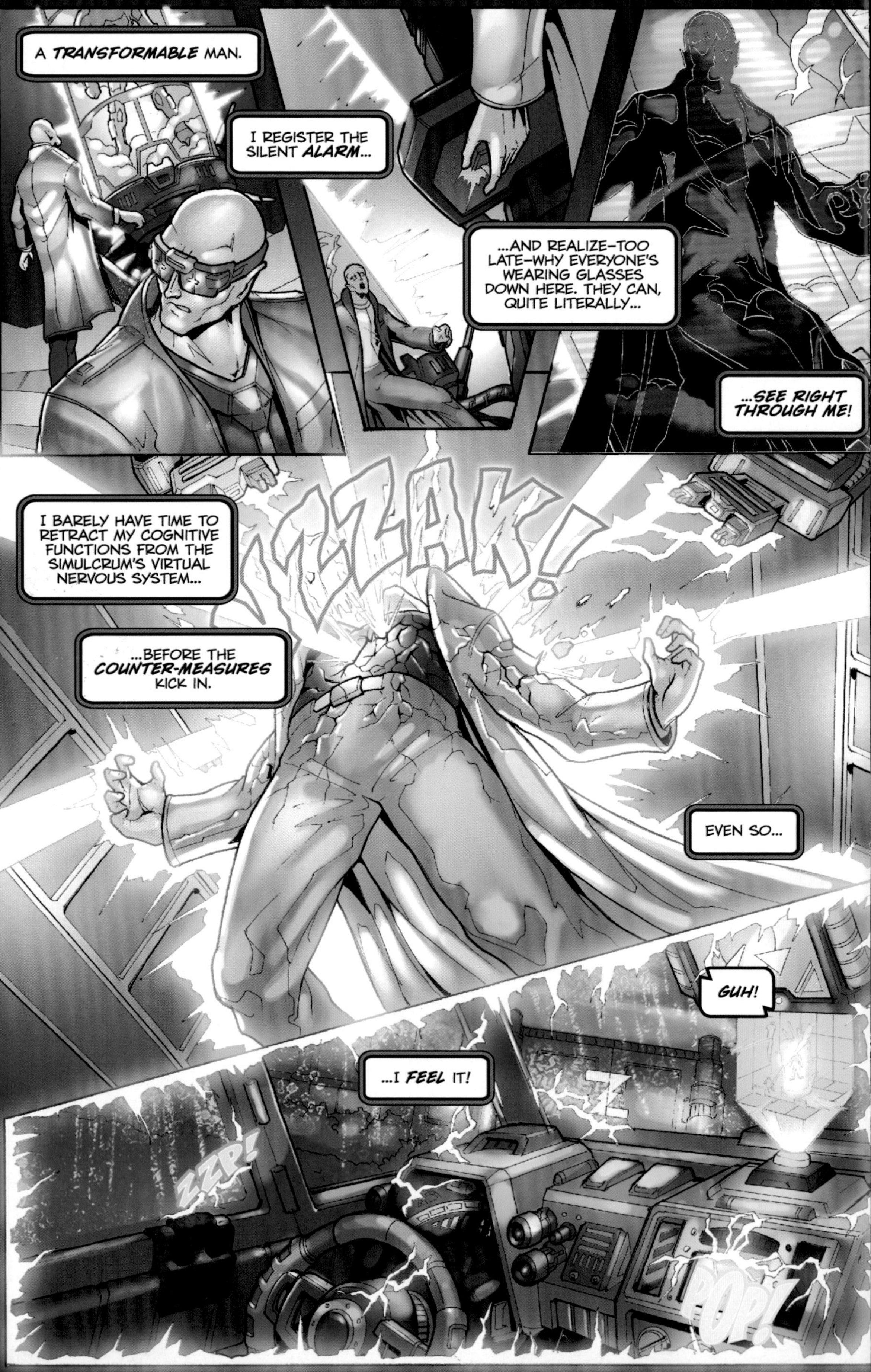
A TRANSFORMABLE MAN.
I REGISTER THE SILENT ALARM...
...AND REALIZE–TOO LATE–WHY EVERYONE'S WEARING GLASSES DOWN HERE. THEY CAN, QUITE LITERALLY...
...SEE RIGHT THROUGH ME!
I BARELY HAVE TIME TO RETRACT MY COGNITIVE FUNCTIONS FROM THE SIMULCRUM'S VIRTUAL NERVOUS SYSTEM...
ZZZAK!
...BEFORE THE COUNTER-MEASURES KICK IN.
EVEN SO...
GUH!
...I FEEL IT!
ZZP!
POP!

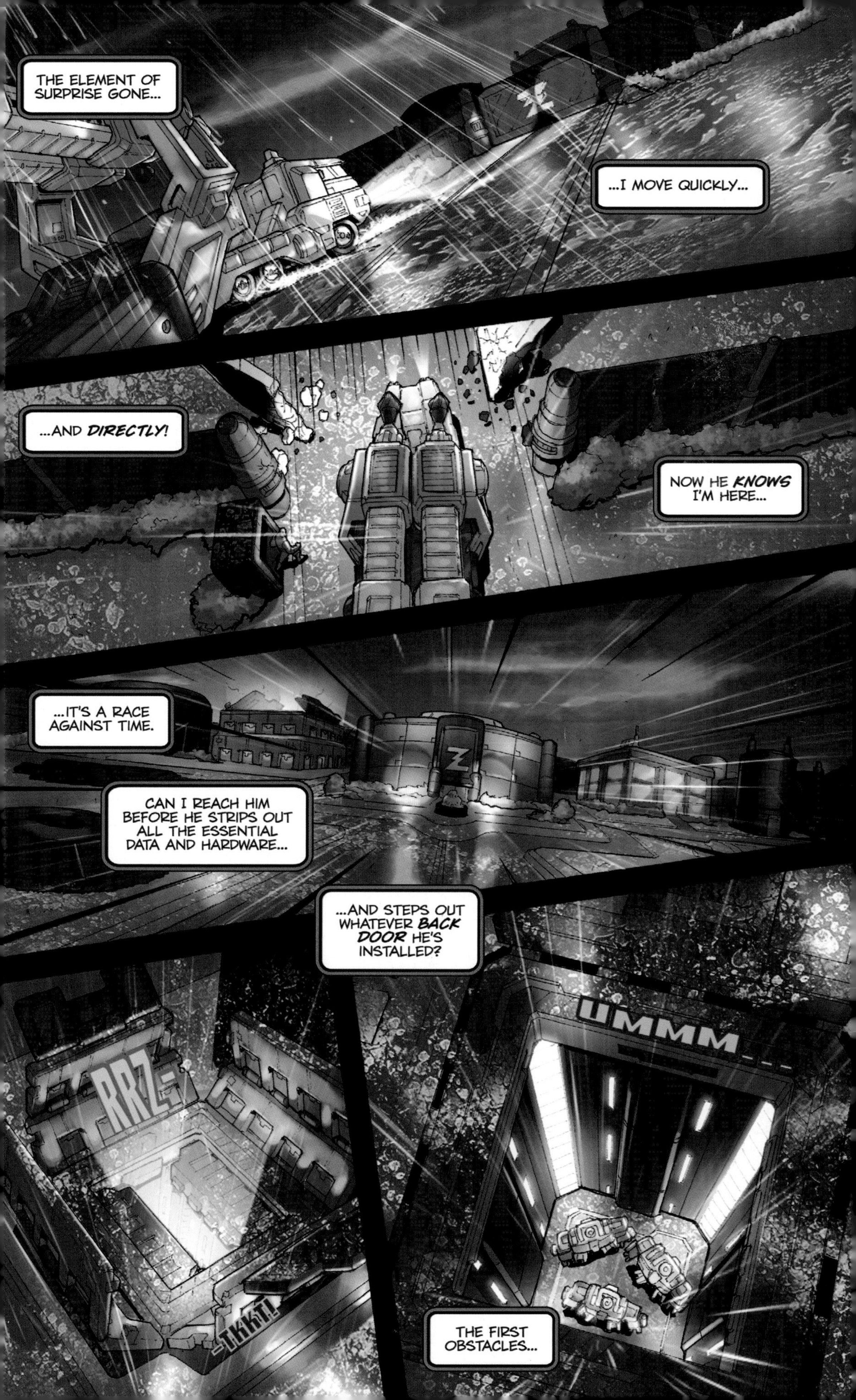
THE ELEMENT OF SURPRISE GONE...
...I MOVE QUICKLY...
...AND DIRECTLY!
NOW HE KNOWS I'M HERE...
...IT'S A RACE AGAINST TIME.
CAN I REACH HIM BEFORE HE STRIPS OUT ALL THE ESSENTIAL DATA AND HARDWARE...
...AND STEPS OUT WHATEVER BACK DOOR HE'S INSTALLED?
RRZ-
UMMMM
TKKT!
THE FIRST OBSTACLES...

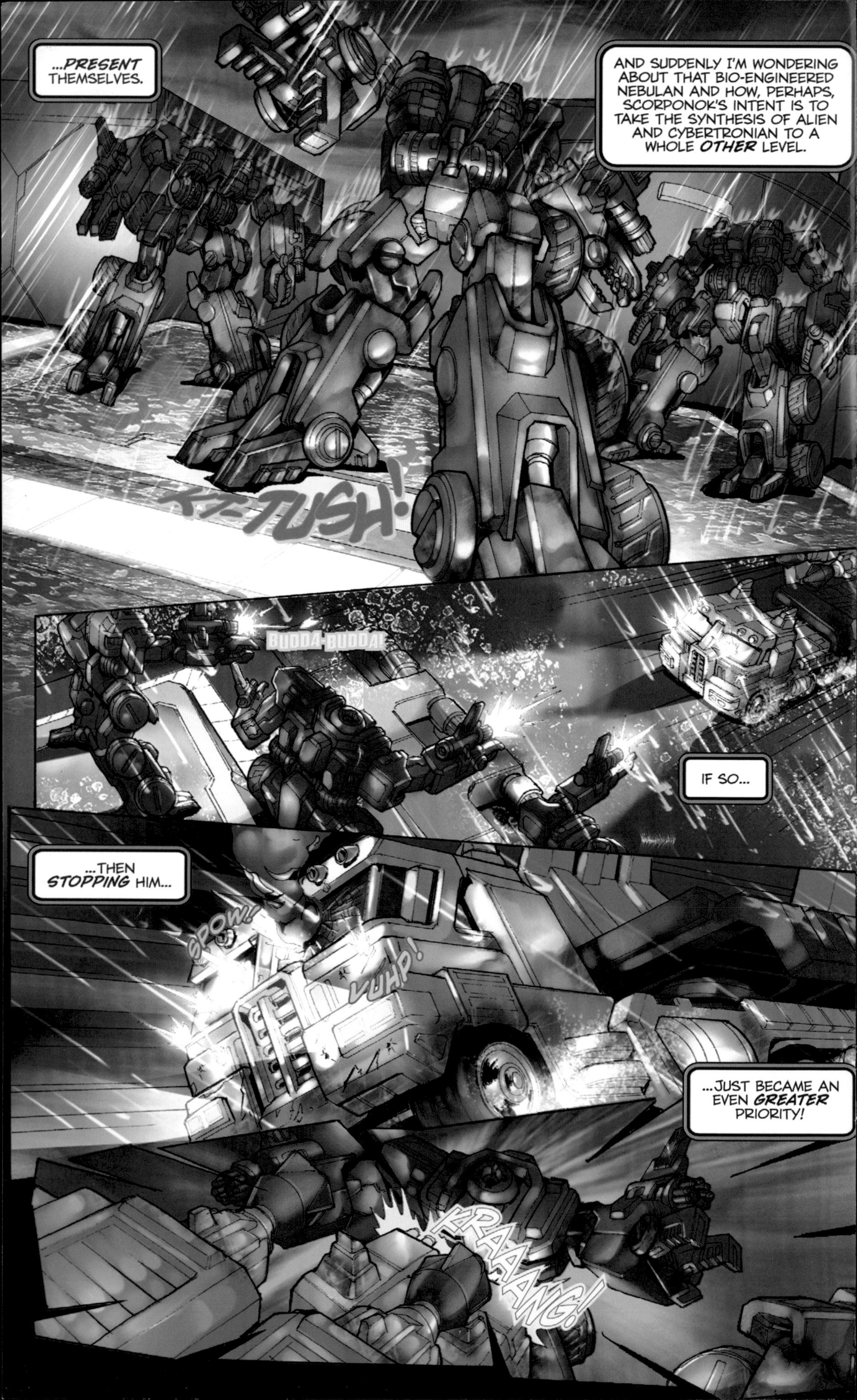
...PRESENT THEMSELVES.
AND SUDDENLY I'M WONDERING ABOUT THAT BIO-ENGINEERED NEBULAN AND HOW, PERHAPS, SCORPONOK'S INTENT IS TO TAKE THE SYNTHESIS OF ALIEN AND CYBERTRONIAN TO A WHOLE OTHER LEVEL.
KT-TUSH!
BUDDA-BUDDA!
IF SO...
...THEN STOPPING HIM...
SPOW!
VUHP!
...JUST BECAME AN EVEN GREATER PRIORITY!
KRAAANG!

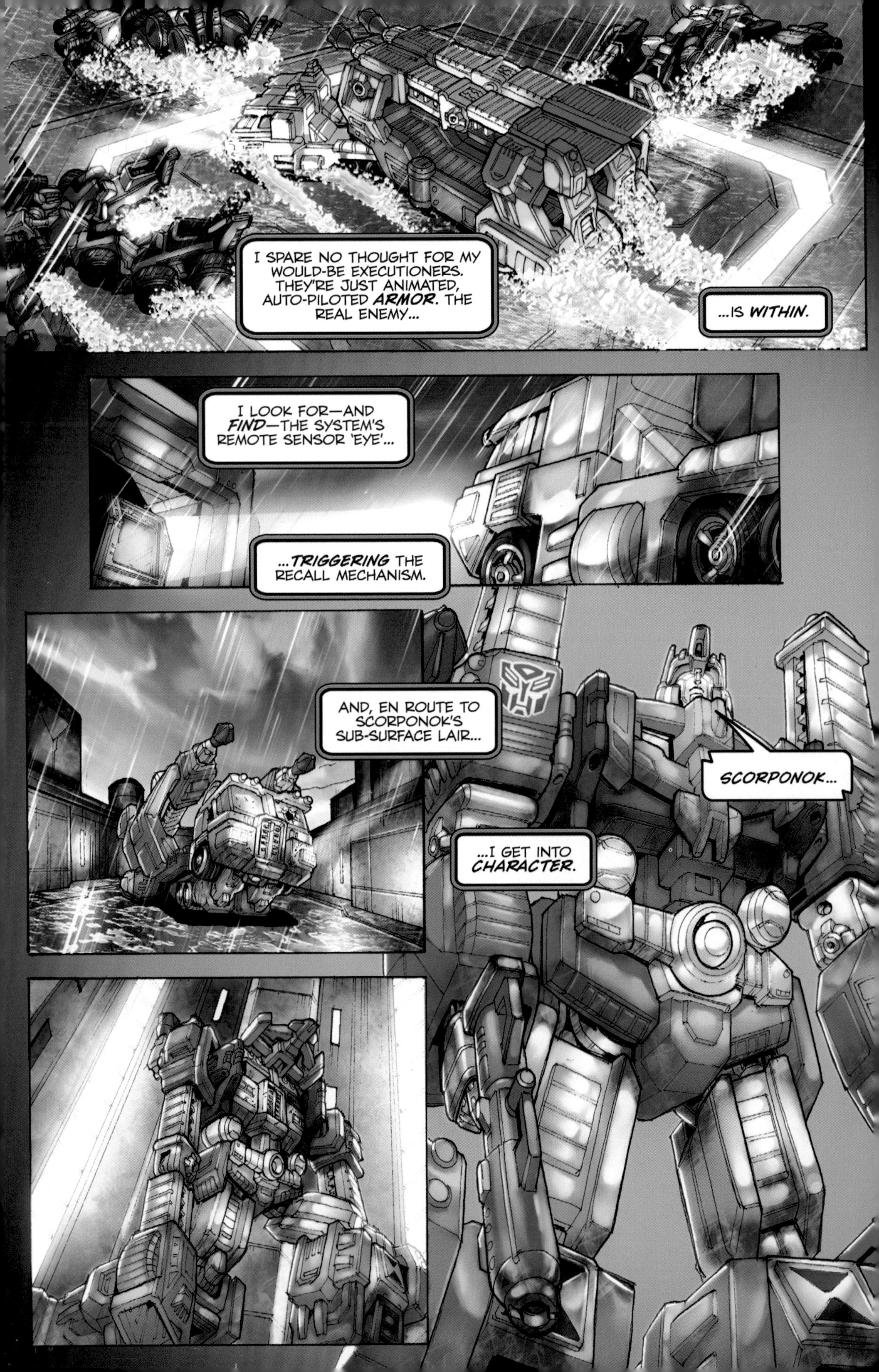
I SPARE NO THOUGHT FOR MY WOULD-BE EXECUTIONERS. THEY'RE JUST ANIMATED, AUTO-PILOTED *ARMOR*. THE REAL ENEMY...
...IS *WITHIN*.
I LOOK FOR—AND *FIND*—THE SYSTEM'S REMOTE SENSOR 'EYE'...
...*TRIGGERING* THE RECALL MECHANISM.
AND, EN ROUTE TO SCORPONOK'S SUB-SURFACE LAIR...
SCORPONOK...
...I GET INTO *CHARACTER*.

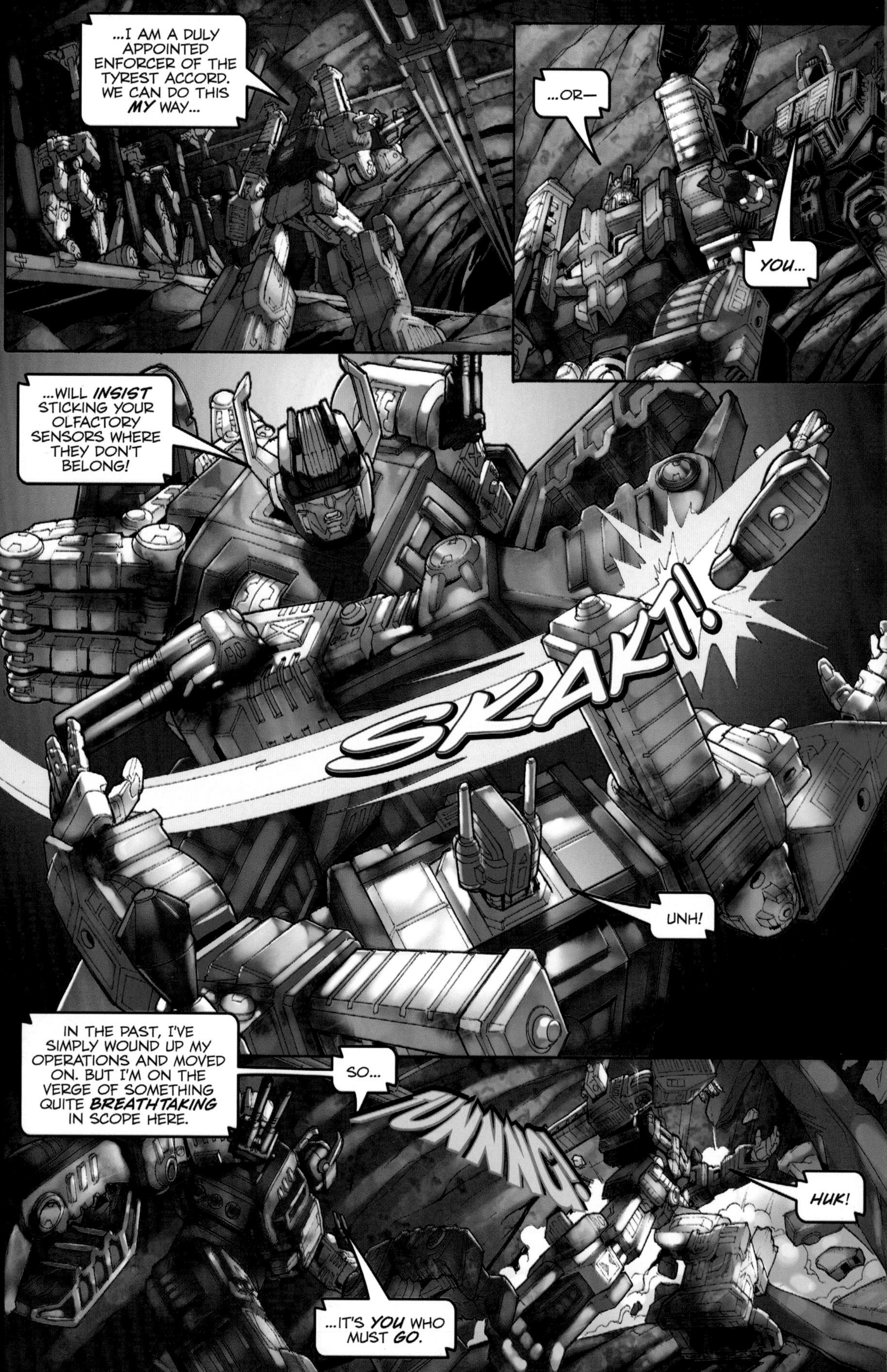

...I AM A DULY APPOINTED ENFORCER OF THE TYREST ACCORD. WE CAN DO THIS *MY* WAY...
...OR—
YOU...
...WILL *INSIST* STICKING YOUR OLFACTORY SENSORS WHERE THEY DON'T BELONG!
SKAKT!!
UNH!
IN THE PAST, I'VE SIMPLY WOUND UP MY OPERATIONS AND MOVED ON. BUT I'M ON THE VERGE OF SOMETHING QUITE *BREATHTAKING* IN SCOPE HERE.
SO...
HUK!
...IT'S *YOU* WHO MUST *GO*.

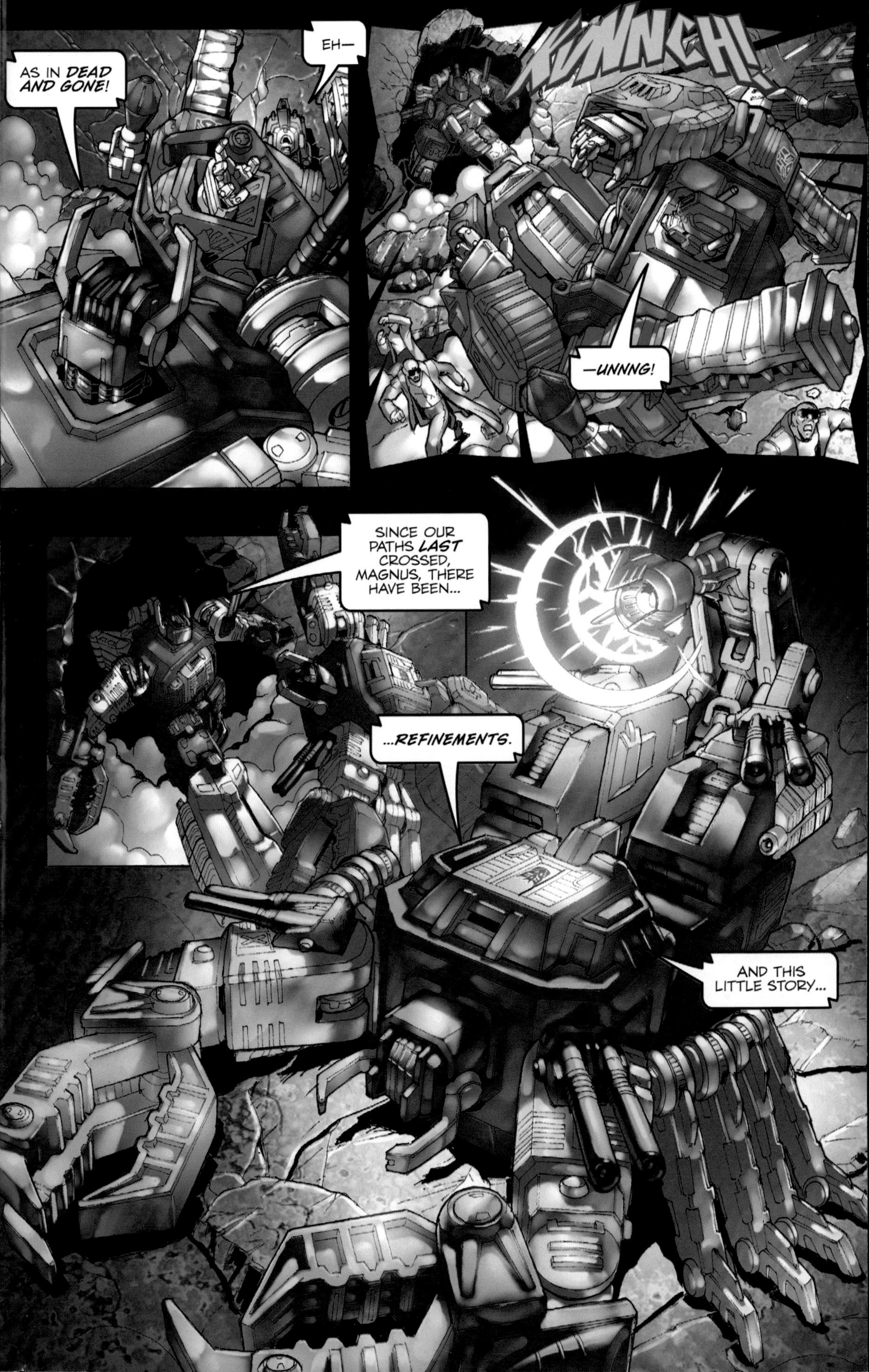

AS IN DEAD AND GONE!
EH—
KUNNCH!
—UNNG!
SINCE OUR PATHS LAST CROSSED, MAGNUS, THERE HAVE BEEN...
...REFINEMENTS.
AND THIS LITTLE STORY...

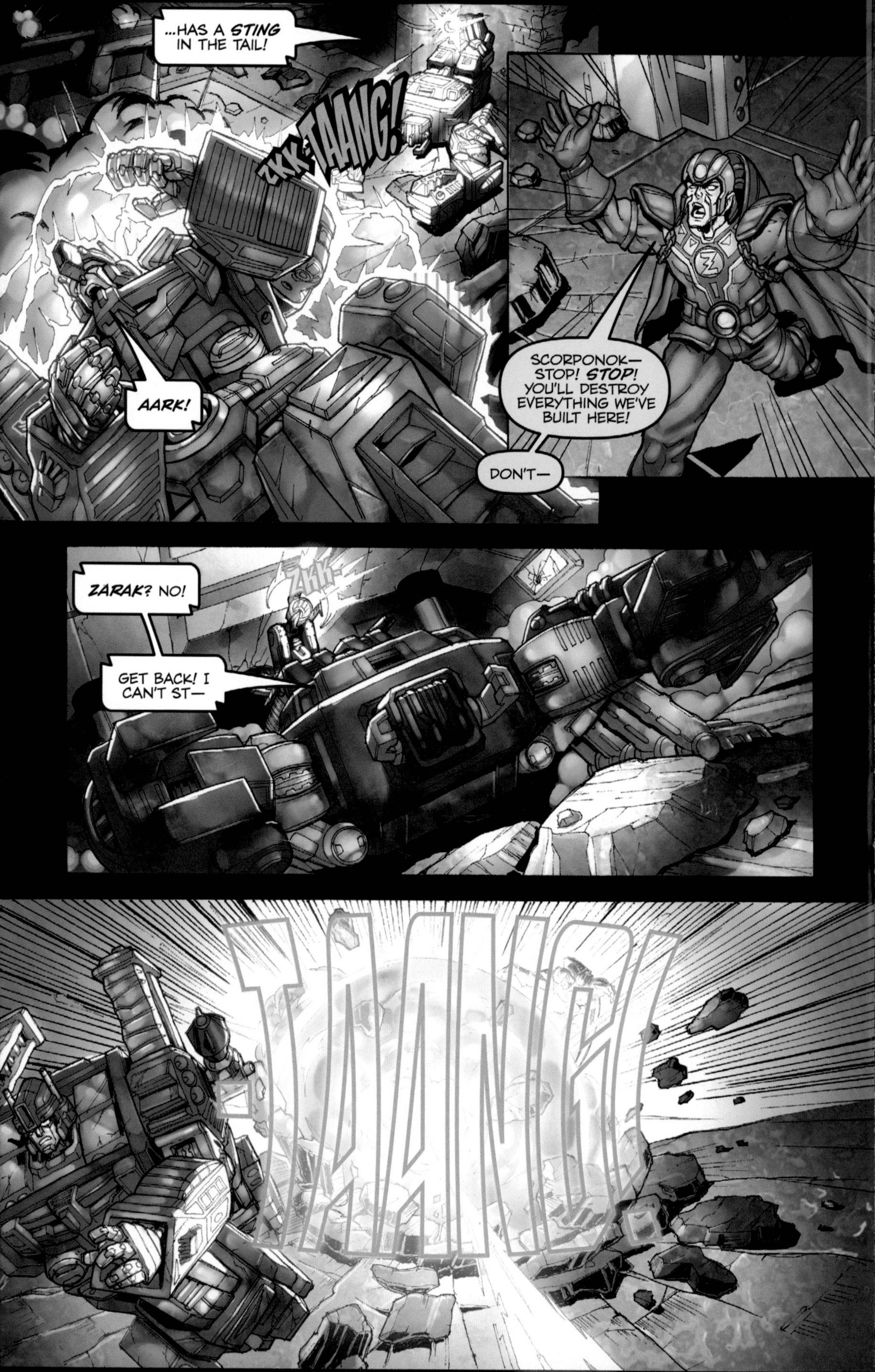
...HAS A *STING* IN THE TAIL!
ZKK-TAANG!
AARK!
SCORPONOK— STOP! ***STOP!*** YOU'LL DESTROY EVERYTHING WE'VE BUILT HERE!
DON'T—
ZARAK? NO!
ZKK-
GET BACK! I CAN'T ST—
TAANG!

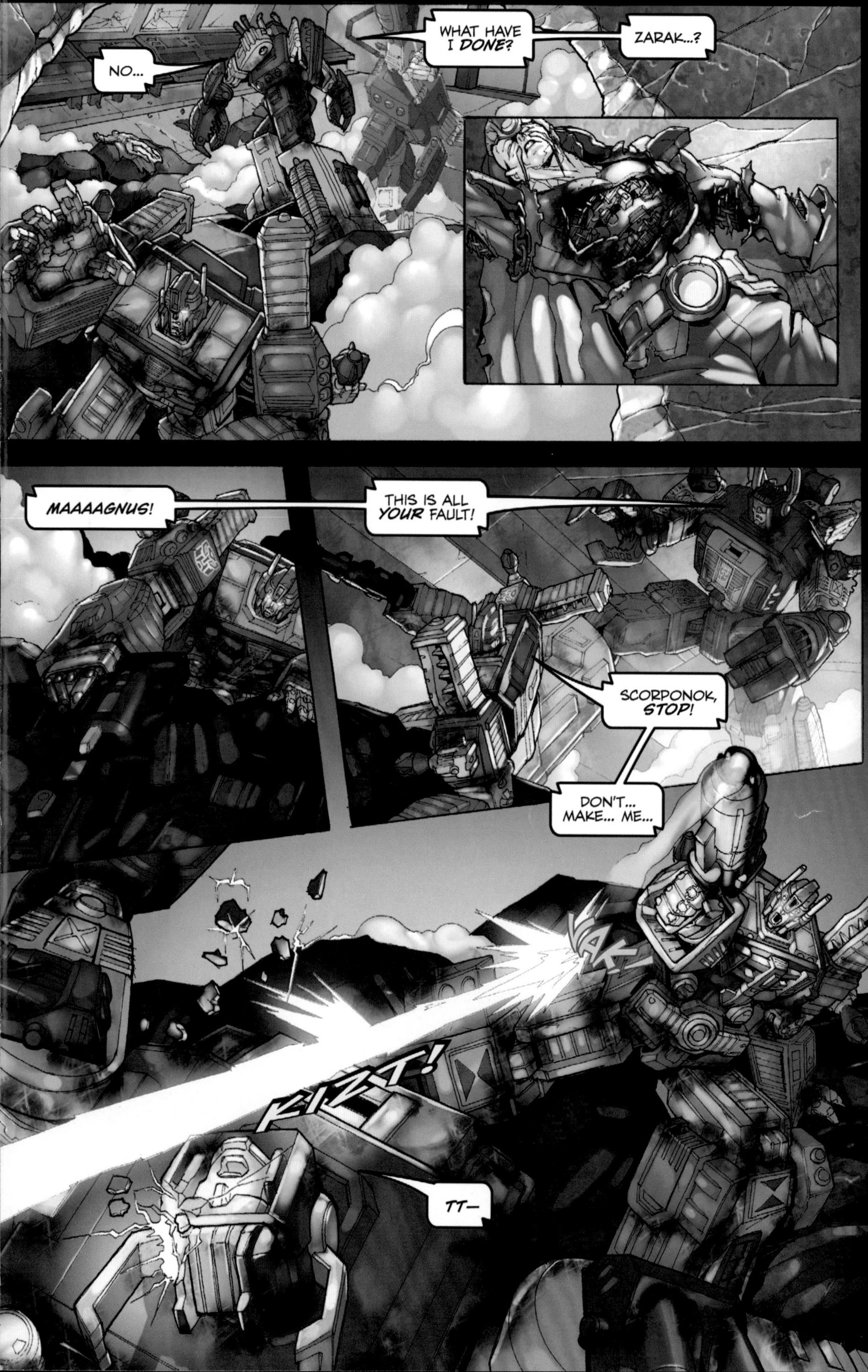
NO...
WHAT HAVE I DONE?
ZARAK...?
MAAAAGNUS!
THIS IS ALL YOUR FAULT!
SCORPONOK, STOP!
DON'T... MAKE... ME...
KIZZT!
TT—

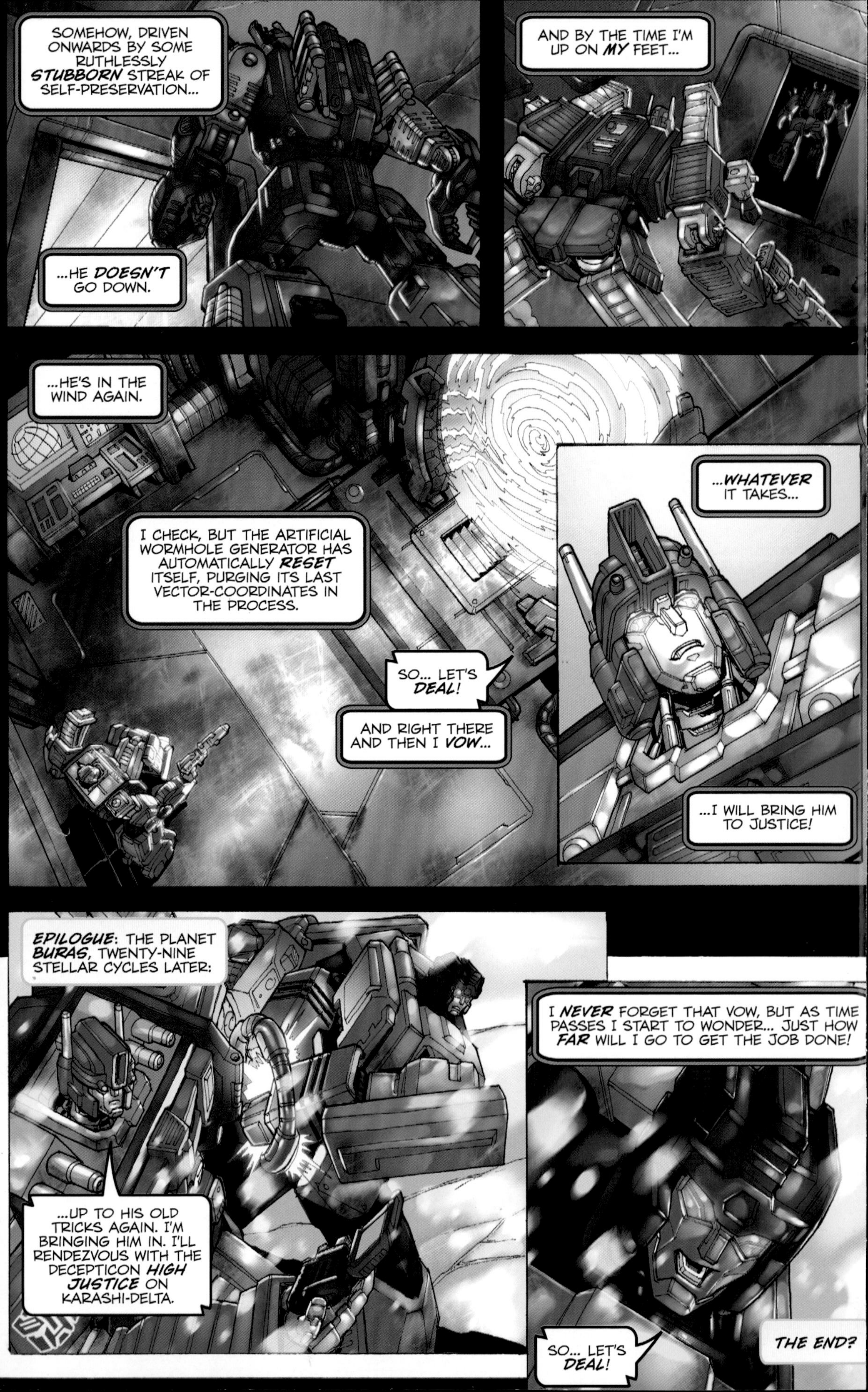
SOMEHOW, DRIVEN ONWARDS BY SOME RUTHLESSLY STUBBORN STREAK OF SELF-PRESERVATION...
...HE DOESN'T GO DOWN.
AND BY THE TIME I'M UP ON MY FEET...
...HE'S IN THE WIND AGAIN.
I CHECK, BUT THE ARTIFICIAL WORMHOLE GENERATOR HAS AUTOMATICALLY RESET ITSELF, PURGING ITS LAST VECTOR-COORDINATES IN THE PROCESS.
SO... LET'S DEAL!
AND RIGHT THERE AND THEN I VOW...
...WHATEVER IT TAKES...
...I WILL BRING HIM TO JUSTICE!
EPILOGUE: THE PLANET BURAS, TWENTY-NINE STELLAR CYCLES LATER:
...UP TO HIS OLD TRICKS AGAIN. I'M BRINGING HIM IN. I'LL RENDEZVOUS WITH THE DECEPTICON HIGH JUSTICE ON KARASHI-DELTA.
I NEVER FORGET THAT VOW, BUT AS TIME PASSES I START TO WONDER... JUST HOW FAR WILL I GO TO GET THE JOB DONE!
SO... LET'S DEAL!
THE END?